We're Very Good Friends, My Grandpa and I

Written and Illustrated
by

P.K. Hallinan

For Fla, with love.

Copyright © 1988 by Patrick K. Hallinan
All rights reserved.
Printed and bound in U.S.A.
Published by Ideals Publishing Corporation
Nelson Place at Elm Hill Pike
Nashville, Tennessee 37214
ISBN 0-8249-8345-9

We're very good friends,
my grandpa and I.

We like to take walks...

And watch cars drive by.

And sometimes he goes
just a little bit slow,
but that's fine with me—
we're good friends, you know.

4

We do lots of neat things,
my grandpa and I.

We cook up French toast;

we go hunting for ghosts.

We laugh with our eyes
about Grandma's burnt roasts.

And sometimes we just sit
and we don't talk at all.
But that's okay, too;
we're friends, after all.

We always have fun,
my grandpa and I.

We whistle to birds
and offer them bread.

We walk to the beach
with our hats on our heads

We even go shopping
and dance down the aisles
with Grandpa's soft-shoe
bringing all kinds of smiles.

And frankly we're happy
to spend the whole day
just being together
in wonderful ways...

like watching TV
with the sound turned way up,

or painting some flowers
on old coffee cups,

or maybe just sorting through
Grandpa's old files
and putting the papers
in six different piles.

We make quite a team,
my grandpa and I.

Then in the evening
it's time for a story—
how Grandpa saved Europe
while waving Old Glory!

19

But if he starts yawning
and takes a short nap,
I just like to stay there
curled up on his lap.

And I know deep inside
he always will be
a part of my heart
with his words guiding me.

For Grandpa is special
in ways that don't end ...

And he knows every secret
of being a friend.

So when all's said and done,
I guess LOVE is why...

we're very good friends,
my grandpa and I.